The Princess
Who Couldn't Cry

Written by Lucy Floyd
Illustrated by Christine Caron

Once there was a beautiful princess.
She was a very happy princess.

But sometimes she was sad. Yet, even when she was sad, she could not cry.

"Why can't she cry?" asked her father, the king.

"Why can't she cry?" asked her mother, the queen.

"Why can't I cry?" asked the beautiful princess. "If I could cry, I would feel better."

So everyone tried to make the beautiful princess cry. They read sad, sad tales.

Everyone cried. The princess looked sad. But she couldn't cry.

So everyone tried again. They played sad, sad tunes.

Everyone cried. The princess looked sad. But she couldn't cry.

"I just can't cry," said the beautiful princess. "I give up!"

"Wait!" said the queen as she jumped up.
"Don't give up. I have a plan."

"What is it?" asked the king.

"Wait and see," said the queen.

"I will jump on my horse. I will go to see the farmer."

And that is what she did.

"Will you help me?" she asked the farmer.
"I need some onions. I am going to play
a little trick on the princess."

"What kind of trick?" asked the farmer.

"Wait and see," said the queen. "I will jump on my horse. Please come with me, and bring the onions."

"I will jump in my cart," said the farmer.
"We will bring the onions with us."

And that is what they did.

"What are you going to do with that onion?" asked the king.

"Wait and see," said the queen. "Here, dear. Cut this!" she said to the princess.

The princess cut the onion. Was this a good trick? Would it work?

As the princess cut the onion, she began crying. Then she cried even more.

"She's crying!" everyone said. They were so happy!

And so was the princess.